For my mother, Lillian
– A. S.

For my mother and father with gratitude
– X. L.

Text copyright © 2000 by Aaron Shepard
Illustrations copyright © 2000 by Xiaojun Li
Chinese translation copyright © 2000 by Pan Asian Publications (USA) Inc.

Published in the United States of America by EduStar Press,
an imprint of Pan Asian Publications (USA) Inc.
29564 Union City Blvd., Union City, CA 94587
Tel. (510) 475-1185   Fax (510) 475-1489

This story first appeared in *Cricket*, 1999, and in Australia's *School Magazine*, 1999.
Cover and jacket design by Xiaojun Li
Book design by Paula Sugarman and Linda Pucilowski,
Sugarman Design Group, LLP
Editorial and production assistance: Art & Publishing Consultants, Montreal

ISBN 1-57227-066-7
Library of Congress Catalog Card Number: 99-69461

Printed by South China Printing Co. (1988) Ltd., Hong Kong

The Magic Brocade

A Tale of China

神奇的織錦

English/Chinese

Retold by Aaron Shepard   Illustrated by Xiaojun Li
Chinese Translation by Isabella Chen

EDUSTAR PRESS

Once in China there lived an old widow and her son, Chen. The widow was known all over for the brocades that she made on her loom. Weaving threads of silver, gold, and colored silk into her cloth, she made pictures of flowers, birds, and animals so real they seemed almost alive. People said there were no brocades finer than the ones the widow wove.

　　從前在中國，有一位老寡婦，她和兒子阿誠相依爲命。老寡婦織得一手好布，手藝遠近馳名。她用金絲銀線各色彩線織成花鳥百獸，圖案栩栩如生。大家都稱讚老寡婦織工細，沒人能跟她比。

One day, the widow took a pile of brocades to the marketplace where she quickly sold them. Then she went about buying her household needs.

All at once she stopped. "Oh, my!" Her eye had been caught by a beautiful painted scroll that hung in one of the stalls. It showed a marvelous palace, all red and yellow and blue and green, reaching delicately to the sky. All around were fantastic gardens and, walking through them, the loveliest maidens.

"Do you like it?" asked the stall keeper. "It's a painting of Sun Palace. They say it lies far to the east and is the home of many fairy ladies."

"It's wonderful," said the widow with a shiver and a sigh. "It makes me want to be there."

　　一天，老寡婦帶著一批織錦到市集去，不一會兒，織錦全賣完了。她便四處逛逛，採買家裡所需的東西。

　　忽然間，她停住腳步，脫口叫道：「天啊！」老寡婦的目光被攤子上掛的一幅畫軸深深吸引——畫中是一座五彩繽紛的宮殿，殿堂高聳參天，四周環繞著綺麗的花園，還有美麗的仙女們漫步其間。

　　「您可中意這幅畫？」攤子的小販問道，「這是天宮圖。相傳它在遙遠的東方，是許多仙女的家。」

　　「多美的一幅畫啊！」彷彿有一道電流通過全身，老寡婦不禁打了個哆嗦，嘆息說：「如果能身歷其境，我便了無遺憾！」

Though it cost most of her money, the widow could not resist buying the scroll. When she got back to her cottage, she showed it to her son. "Look, Chen. Have you ever seen anything more beautiful? How I would love to live in that palace, or at least visit it!"

Chen looked at her thoughtfully. "Mother, why don't you weave the picture as a brocade? That would be almost like being there."

"Why, Chen, what a marvelous idea! I'll start at once."

She set up her loom and began to weave. She worked for hours, then days, then weeks, barely stopping to eat or sleep. Her eyes grew bloodshot, and her fingers raw.

"Mother," said Chen anxiously, "shouldn't you get more rest?"

"Oh, Chen, it's so hard to stop. While I weave, I feel like I'm there at Sun Palace. And I don't want to come away!"

Because the widow no longer wove brocades to sell, Chen cut firewood and sold that instead. Months went by, while inch by inch the pattern appeared on the loom.

雖然幾乎得花光身上的銀兩，老寡婦還是忍不住把畫買下來。一回到家，老寡婦迫不及待將畫拿給兒子看。「阿誠，你看過這麼美的畫嗎？如果能住在天宮裡該有多好，起碼也讓我親眼瞧瞧！」

阿誠邊看邊想，說道：「娘，您為什麼不將這幅畫織成織錦，這麼一來不就如同身歷其境？」

「哎呀，真是好主意，我這就織布去！」

老寡婦架起織布機，動手織起天宮圖。幾個時辰、幾個晝夜、幾個星期過去，老寡婦不吃也不睡，織到眼睛紅腫、手指也磨破了。

「娘，」阿誠看在眼裡、急在心裡，「您怎麼不多歇會兒？」

「阿誠啊，娘停不下來，只要織著織著，就彷彿到了天宮，一步也不想離開。」

就這樣，老寡婦不再拿織錦到市集賣，家中生計全靠阿誠砍柴。幾個月過去，天宮圖一寸一寸浮現在織布機上。

One day, Chen came in to find the loom empty and the widow sobbing. "What's wrong, Mother?" he asked in alarm.

She looked at him tearfully. "I've finished it."

The brocade was laid out on the floor. And there it all was—the palace reaching to the sky, the beautiful gardens, the lovely fairy ladies.

"It looks so real," said Chen in amazement. "I feel like I could step into it!" Just then, a sudden wind whipped through the cottage. It lifted the brocade, blew it out the window, and carried it through the air. The widow and her son rushed outside, only to watch the brocade disappear into the east.

"It's gone!" cried the widow, and she fainted away.

　　一天，阿誠回到家，發現織布機上空無一物，只見老寡婦在一旁哽咽。「娘，怎麼了？」他焦急地問。

　　老寡婦淚流滿面地答道：「我把天宮圖織好了！」

　　果然，鋪在地上的織錦，呈現著高聳的宮殿、綺麗的花園和美麗的仙女。

　　「實在太逼真了，」阿誠不由得讚歎，「彷彿一腳就可以踏入天宮裡！」

　　說時遲那時快，忽然一陣風吹進屋裏，將天宮錦飄然捲起，往窗外的天空飛去。老寡婦和阿誠奪門而出，卻只能眼睜睜看著天宮錦，消失在東方的天際。

　　「它不見了！」老寡婦大叫一聲便昏了過去。

Chen carried her to her bed and sat beside her for many hours. At last her eyes opened.

"Chen," she said weakly, "you must find the brocade and bring it back. I cannot live without it."

"Don't worry, Mother. I'll go at once."

Chen gathered a few things and started off toward the east. He walked for hours, then days, then weeks. But there was no sign of the brocade.

阿誠將母親抱回床上，守了好幾個時辰，老寡婦終於睜開雙眼。

「阿誠啊，你得幫娘找回天宮錦，它可是我的命！」老寡婦有氣無力地說。

「娘，您別擔心，我這就動身。」

阿誠收拾了簡單的行李朝東方去。幾個時辰，幾個晝夜，幾個星期過去，還是沒有天宮錦的消息。

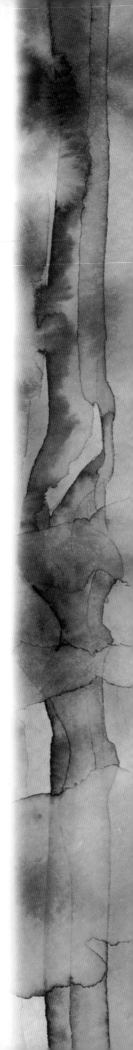

One day, Chen came upon a lonely hut. Sitting by the door was an old, leather-skinned woman smoking a pipe. A horse was grazing nearby. "Hello, deary," said the woman. "What brings you so far from home?"

"I'm looking for my mother's brocade. The wind carried it to the east."

"Ah, yes," said the woman. "The brocade of Sun Palace! Well, that wind was sent by the fairy ladies of the palace itself. They're using the brocade as a pattern for their weaving."

"But my mother will die without it!"

"Well, then, you had best get it back! But you won't get to Sun Palace by foot, so you'd better ride my horse. It will show you the way."

"Thank you!" said Chen.

"Oh, don't thank me yet, deary. Between here and there, you must pass through the flames of Fiery Mountain. If you make a single sound of complaint, you'll be burnt to ashes. After that, you must cross the Icy Sea. The smallest word of discontent, and you'll be frozen solid. Do you still want to go?"

"I must get back my mother's brocade."

"Good boy. Take the horse and go."

　　一天，阿誠來到一處荒野中的茅屋。一個滿臉皺紋的老婦人，坐在門前抽著煙袋，還有一匹馬兒在一邊吃草。

　　「好孩子，」老婦人問道：「什麼風把你吹到這麼遠的地方來？」

　　「我娘的織錦被風吹到東方，爲了它我四處探訪。」

　　「這樣啊！」老婦人說：「你說的是天宮錦？那是仙女差遣的風，爲的是把織錦帶回宮，好當織錦的圖案用。」

　　「可是少了天宮錦，就像要了母親的命！」

　　「既然如此，你最好快快把它要回來。可是你徒步到不了天宮，不如我的馬兒讓你騎，牠知道去天宮的途徑。」

　　「謝謝您！」阿誠說。

　　「先別謝我，孩子。在到達天宮前，你得熬過怒山的火焰，如果稍有怨言，你會被燒成灰燼。就算越過怒山，你還得捱過冰海，只要有一句埋怨，你將會凍爲冰柱。告訴我，你還是執意前往？」

　　「就算得穿越怒山冰海，我也要將天宮錦找回來。」

　　「好孩子，你這就騎馬上路吧！」

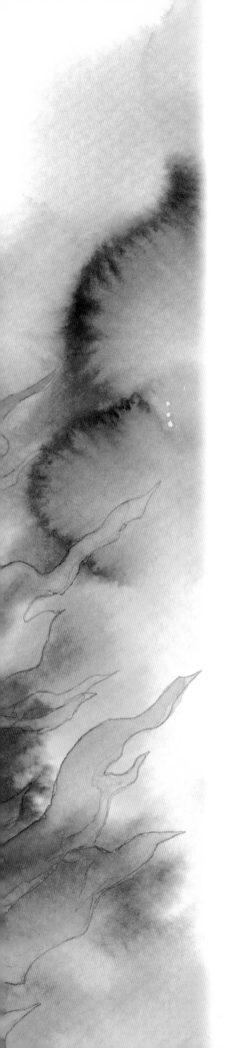

Chen climbed on, and the horse broke into a gallop. Before long they came to a mountain all on fire. Without missing a step, the horse started up the slope, leaping through the flames. Chen felt the fire singe his skin, but he bit his lip and made not a sound.

At last they came down the other side. When they had left the flames behind, Chen was surprised to find that his burns were gone.

阿誠躍上馬背飛奔而去，不久就來到大火熊熊的怒山前。馬兒一步也不停留，在火焰中跳躍著往山上奔去。烈火燒灼著阿誠的皮膚，他只是咬緊牙根不發一語。

終於，阿誠和馬兒翻過山頭下山。一遠離怒山的火焰，阿誠驚訝地發現，身上的灼傷全都消失不見。

A little later, they came to a sea filled with great chunks of ice. Without pausing a moment, the horse began leaping from one ice floe to another. Waves showered them with icy spray, so that Chen was soaked and shivering. But he held his tongue and said not a word.

Finally they reached the far shore. At once, Chen felt himself dry and warm.

過一會兒，他們來到佈滿浮冰的冰海。馬兒一刻也不等待，從一塊浮冰跳上另一塊。冰冷的浪濤潑得阿誠全身濕透、凍得直發抖，他還是閉緊嘴巴，一個字也不說。

他們好不容易到達對岸。立刻，阿誠的衣服乾了、身子也暖了。

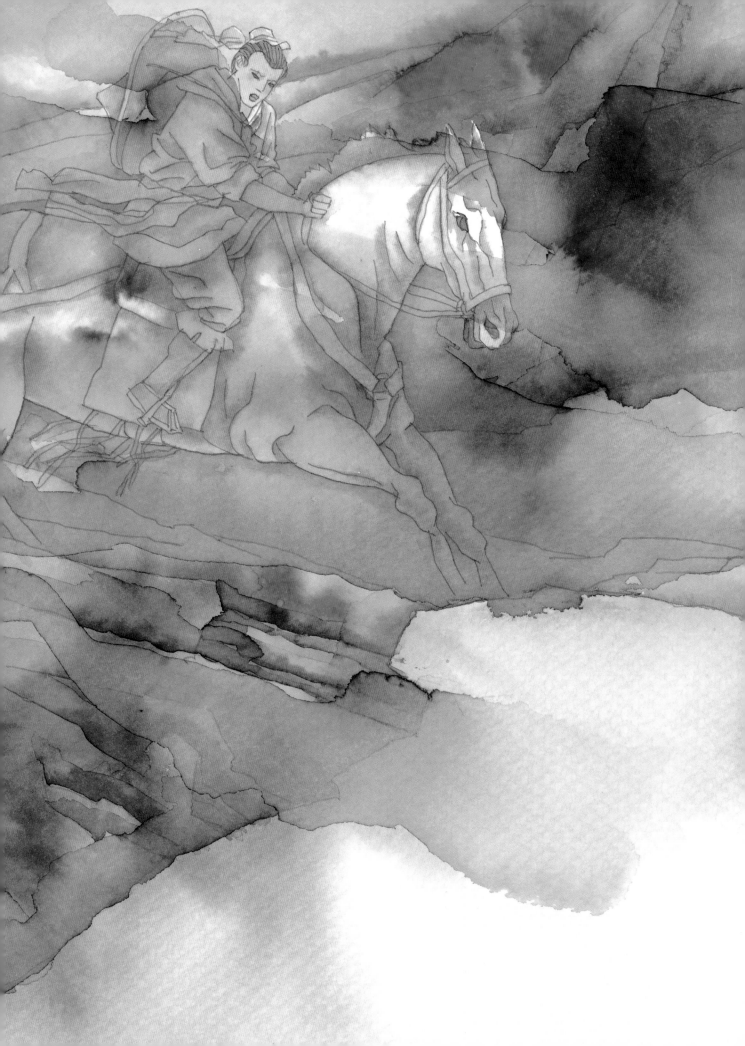

It wasn't long then till they came to Sun Palace. It looked just like his mother's brocade! He rode to the entrance, sprang from the horse, and hurried into a huge hall. Sitting there at looms were dozens of fairy ladies, who turned to stare at him, then whispered to each other excitedly. On each loom was a copy of his mother's brocade, and the brocade itself hung in the center of the room.

　　沒有多久，他們終於到達天宮。眼前的景象正和老寡婦織錦的圖案一模一樣！阿誠在殿前跳下馬，快步走入大廳。廳裏的仙女們坐在一架架織布機前，一看見他便轉頭竊竊私語。每架織布機上的織錦都模仿著老寡婦織的圖案，天宮錦則高掛在大廳正中央。

A lady near the door rose from her loom to meet him. "My name is Li-en, and I welcome you. You are the first mortal ever to reach our palace. What good fortune brings you here?"

The fairy was so beautiful that for a moment Chen could only stare. Li-en gazed shyly downward. "Dear lady, I have come for my mother's brocade."

"So you are the widow's son!" said Li-en. "How we admire that brocade! None of us has been able to match it. We wish to keep it here till we can."

"But I must bring it home, or my mother will die!"

Li-en looked alarmed, and a flurry of whispers arose in the room. She stepped away to speak softly with several others, then returned to Chen. "We surely must not let that happen to her. Only let us keep the brocade for the rest of the day, so we can try to finish our own. Tomorrow you may take it back with you."

"Thank you, dear lady," said Chen.

門邊一位仙女起身迎向阿誠。「歡迎歡迎，我是蓮仙。來到天宮的凡人，你是第一個。你真是幸運！」

一見這麼美麗的仙女，阿誠看得發呆，蓮仙害羞地低下頭來。

「仙女，我是為我娘的天宮錦而來。」

「原來你就是老寡婦的兒子！」蓮仙說：「你母親的天宮錦太令人讚賞，這裡的仙女沒人比得上，我們暫時借來當作圖案，等到學會必定立刻奉還。」

「但是我若不把織錦帶回家，母親恐怕活不下！」

蓮仙吃了一驚，廳裏響起嗡嗡的耳語聲。蓮仙和仙女們低聲商量後，轉身告訴阿誠：「我們絕不能讓這種事發生。天宮錦今天還是留在這兒，我們盡量織完自己的圖案。明天你就可以把它帶走。」

「謝謝仙女。」阿誠說。

The fairies worked busily to finish their brocades. Chen sat near Li-en at her loom. As she wove, he told her about his life in the human world, and she told him about hers at Sun Palace. Many smiles and glances passed between them.

When darkness fell, the fairies worked on by the light of a magic pearl. At last Chen's eyes would stay open no longer, and he drifted to sleep on his chair.

One by one the fairies finished or left off, and went out of the hall. Li-en was the last one there, and it was almost dawn when she was done. She cut her brocade from the loom and held it beside the widow's. She sighed. "Mine is good, but the widow's is still better. If only she could come and teach us herself."

Then Li-en had an idea. With needle and thread, she embroidered a small image onto the widow's brocade—an image of herself on the palace steps. She softly said a spell. Then she left the hall, with a last long smiling gaze at Chen.

　　仙女們忙著完成織錦，阿誠在蓮仙的織布機旁坐下。蓮仙一邊織，一邊聽阿誠敘述他在人間的生活，蓮仙也談她在天宮的種種。聊到投緣處，兩人不由得相視而笑。

　　入夜之後，仙女在夜明珠的光華中繼續趕工。阿誠覺得眼皮越來越重，終於靠在椅子上沈沈睡去。

　　有人完成了，有人放棄了。仙女們一個接一個離去，最後只剩蓮仙還在廳裏。等她織完，天都快亮了。她將織錦由織布機取下，掛在老寡婦的天宮錦旁。蓮仙嘆道：「雖然我已經織得很好，但是老寡婦手藝更精妙。如果她能親自來教我們，那該有多好！」

　　這時，蓮仙想到一個主意。她拿起針線，在天宮錦裏繡了一個小小的人像—蓮仙自己站在殿階上的模樣。她輕輕念了一句咒語，含笑望了望阿誠，才轉身離去。

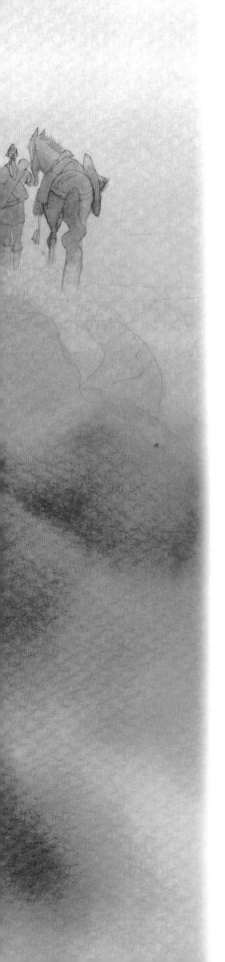

When Chen woke up, the sun was just rising. He looked around the hall for Li-en, but saw no one. Though he longed to find her to say good-bye, he told himself, "I must not waste a moment."

He rolled up his mother's brocade, rushed from the hall, and jumped onto the horse. Back he raced, across the Icy Sea and over Fiery Mountain.

When he reached the old woman's hut, she was standing there waiting for him. "Hurry, Chen! Your mother is dying! Put on these shoes, or you'll never get there in time."

Chen put them on. One step, two, three, then he was racing over the countryside faster than he could believe possible. In no time, he was home.

阿誠醒來時，太陽剛剛升起。他四下尋找蓮仙，想親自向她道別，可惜大廳裡空無一人。阿誠提醒自己：「我一刻都耽擱不得。」他捲起母親的天宮錦，匆匆走出大廳，躍上馬背出發，再一次渡過冰海，越過怒山，趕路回家。

當他們回到荒野的茅屋前，老婦人已經等候多時，「快，阿誠，你母親命在旦夕，趕緊換上這雙鞋，否則你會趕不及。」

阿誠套上了鞋，一步、兩步、三步，他飛奔著穿過原野，速度快得難以置信。不一會兒他就回到家門前。

He rushed into the cottage and found the widow in bed, pale and quiet. "Mother!"

Her eyes opened slowly. "Chen?"

"Mother, I brought it." He unrolled the cloth onto the bed.

"My brocade!" The widow raised herself to look. Color came back to her face, and she seemed already stronger. "Chen, I need more light. Let's take it outside."

He helped her out of the cottage and placed the brocade on a rock. But just then a sudden wind came, and the brocade rose slowly in the air. It stretched as it rose, growing larger and larger, till it filled their view completely. The palace was as large as Chen himself had seen it, and standing on the steps was the fairy lady Li-en.

阿誠衝進屋裏，看見蒼白的母親躺在床上，「娘！」

老寡婦慢慢張開眼，「阿誠，是你嗎？」

「娘，我把天宮錦帶回來了。」阿誠將織錦攤在床前。

「我的天宮錦！」老寡婦掙扎起身端詳，血色逐漸回到臉上，身子也變得硬朗。

「阿誠啊，屋裏太暗，咱們到外頭看！」

阿誠扶著老寡婦走到屋外，將織錦鋪在大石塊上。這時，一陣風忽然吹來，天宮錦隨風緩緩升起，向四方徐徐展開，直到映滿了他們的眼簾。宏偉的天宮一如阿誠親眼所見，殿階上站的正是蓮仙。

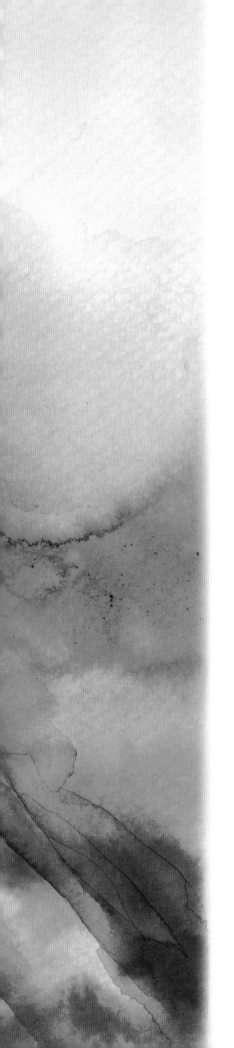

Li-en was beckoning with her hand. "Quickly!" she called. "While the wind still blows! Step into the brocade!"

For a moment, Chen was too astounded to move. Then he took hold of his mother's arm, and together they stepped forward. There was a shimmering, and there they stood before Sun Palace.

蓮仙向他們母子招手，喊：「快！趁著風還在吹，快站到天宮錦裏來！」

阿誠大吃一驚，好一會兒動彈不得。等他回過神，攙著母親的手臂一起跨步向前。一道亮光閃過，他們已經站在天宮前。

Li-en rushed up to them, and the other fairies gathered around. She said to the widow, "Welcome, honored one. If it pleases you, we wish you to live with us and teach us the secrets of your craft."

"Nothing could please me more!" cried the widow. "But, Chen, is it all right with you?"

Chen looked in Li-en's eyes and smiled. "Yes, Mother, it's just fine with me."

So the widow became teacher to the fairies, and Chen became husband to Li-en. And people say there are no brocades finer than the ones they weave at Sun Palace.

　　蓮仙趕上來迎接他們，仙女們也跟著圍過來。蓮仙對老寡婦說：「歡迎您大駕光
臨。如果您不嫌棄，請您留在宮裏，傳授我們織錦的訣竅。」
　　「我高興都來不及！」老寡婦喜極而泣：「只不過，孩子啊，你可願意？」
　　阿誠看著蓮仙，眼裡充滿笑意，「是的，娘，我當然願意！」
　　從此老寡婦成為仙女們的織錦老師，阿誠也和蓮仙結為夫妻。大家都說：「天宮
仙女織工細，錦中天地無人及！」

How to say the names

Chen **CHEN**
Li-en **lee-EN**

About the Story

This tale is retold from "The Piece of Chuang Brocade" in *Folk Tales from China,* Third Series, Foreign Languages Press, Peking, 1958.

Brocade is woven cloth with raised patterns resembling embroidery. Though often confused with tapestry, it is made in an entirely different way. Brocade has been woven in China since at least the third century. There it is used for waistcoats, quilt covers, bedspreads, and other household items.

About the Author

 Aaron Shepard is the award-winning author of more than twenty retellings of traditional literature from around the world. His work has been honored by the American Library Association, the National Council for the Social Studies, and the American Folklore Society. Aaron also provides a multitude of resources for teachers and librarians at his website, *www.aaronshep.com*. He lives in the Los Angeles area.

About the Illustrator

 Xiaojun Li is an internationally known children's book illustrator. His work has won him awards in China, Japan, and the United States. Mr. Li was born and raised in Inner Mongolia, China. He now lives with his wife and son in Davis, California.